Disney's

HERCULES

ADAPTED BY
Cathy East Dubowski

ADAPTED FROM
WALT DISNEY PICTURES' **HERCULES**
MUSIC BY ALAN MENKEN   LYRICS BY DAVID ZIPPEL   ORIGINAL SCORE BY ALAN MENKEN
SCREENPLAY BY RON CLEMENTS & JOHN MUSKER, BOB SHAW & DON McENERY
AND IRENE MECCHI
PRODUCED BY ALICE DEWEY AND JOHN MUSKER & RON CLEMENTS
DIRECTED BY JOHN MUSKER & RON CLEMENTS
DISTRIBUTED BY BUENA VISTA PICTURES DISTRIBUTION © DISNEY ENTERPRISES, INC.

Disney
PRESS

New York

SPECIAL EDITION

Library of Congress Catalog Card Number: 96-71630

ISBN:0-7868-4196-6

HERCULES

PROLOGUE

"Long ago, in the faraway land of ancient Greece, there was a golden age of powerful gods and extraordinary heroes.

"And the greatest and strongest of all these heroes was the mighty Hercules. But what is the measure of a true hero? Ah, that is what our story is about—"

"Hey, Narrator!" a voice interrupted. "Lighten up, dude!"

The Narrator stopped and looked around. Who said that?

All he saw was a Grecian urn with the images of five lovely women painted on the side.

"Will you listen to him?" another voice remarked. "He's making this story sound like some Greek tragedy!"

The Narrator gasped as the figures on the vase squirmed to life.

"We'll take it from here, darling," cooed the one named Calliope.

"You go, girl!" the Narrator said. Then he sat back to listen to *their* version of the ancient Greek myth.

Calliope winked and fluffed her hair. "We"—she jerked a thumb at her friends Thalia, Terpsichore, Melpomene, and Clio—"are the Muses. Goddesses of the arts and proclaimers of heroes!"

"Heroes like Hercules," Terpsichore added with a sigh.

Thalia fanned herself. "Honey, you mean *Hunk*-ules!" She leaped from her spot on the vase and tiptoed around to the other side. It was decorated with a dashing portrait of Hercules—a tall handsome hero with muscles to spare.

"Our story," Calliope continued, "actually begins long *before* Hercules.

"Long ago, when the world was new, planet Earth was experiencing more than its fair share of bad luck. Giant brutes called Titans inhabited the planet and they roamed the countryside, causing all kinds of natural disasters— earthquakes, volcanoes, floods. Honey, you name the cata-strophe, those Titans were to blame for it."

"But a strong young god named Zeus came along and defeated the Titans," Terpsichore explained. "Then he locked those suckers in a prison beneath the sea—and sealed it with thunderbolts."

"And that's the gospel truth," Thalia chimed in.

"After that," Calliope went on, "Zeus ruled the universe, and life on Earth was sweet—for a while...."

"Are we coming to the part about Hercules?" Thalia asked dreamily.

Calliope nodded. "You know it, girlfriend."

"Hallelujah!" Thalia squealed.

She quickly took a seat on the rim of the vase and zipped her lip. She didn't want to miss a single word....

CHAPTER I

Mount Olympus, Ancient Greece

"Hercules! Behave yourself!"

Inside Zeus's palace, the goddess Hera shook her head and smiled down at her newborn son. She couldn't *really* be cross with him. He was so adorable! Only hours old, he was a blond, blue-eyed bundle of mischief. His cradle shook as he kicked, waved, and wriggled around.

The mighty Zeus—ruler of all the universe—chuckled. "Look how cute he is!" He reached down to tickle his son. "Kootchy-kootchy-koo!"

Hercules grabbed hold of his daddy's finger—just like any mortal baby on Earth might do.

But Hercules was no ordinary baby. With a tiny coo, he lifted his powerful father straight up in the air!

"He's strong!" Zeus exclaimed proudly. "Just like his dad."

Laughter rippled through the crowd. For it was a joyful day on Mount Olympus, home of the gods, which floated like an island in the clouds above Earth. Celestial fireworks lit the sky. The nectar of the gods flowed. And everyone was there, from Poseidon, god of the sea, to Athena, goddess of wisdom.

Just then Hermes, the messenger god, flew in on winged feet. With a bow, he presented Hera with a bouquet of flowers.

Hera breathed in their lovely scent. "Why, Hermes, they're lovely!"

Hermes smiled and shoved his jazzy glasses up on his nose. "Fabulous party!" he told Zeus.

While the grown-ups talked, baby Hercules stared at the lightning bolts swinging from his father's belt. After several tries he finally caught one in his chubby little hand.

"Better keep those away from the baby, dear," Hera warned.

"Aw, he won't hurt himself," Zeus insisted. "Let the kid have a little fun."

Hercules did what any baby would do: he stuck the lightning bolt in his mouth.

Zap! The jolt fried his baby curls to a crisp. His face crumpled into a pout, and he hurled the bolt out of his crib.

Gods and goddesses leaped out of the way.

Quickly Athena drew her sword and turned the bolt aside, which sent it slicing through the clouds toward Earth.

Now baby Hercules clapped his hands and cooed in delight.

Then Zeus waved for the crowd's attention. "On behalf of my son, I want to thank you all for your wonderful gifts!"

The crowd clapped.

Hera tugged on Zeus's sleeve. "What about our gift, dear?"

"Oh, yes!" Zeus held out his mighty hands. With a flick of the wrist, he began to spin puffs of clouds between his palms.

Baby Hercules watched, spellbound, as a cloud figure slowly formed in his father's huge hands.

It was a pony with wings!

"His name is Pegasus," Zeus said. "He's all yours, Son."

Baby Hercules reached for the little horse. Then the animal opened his eyes and shook cloud bits from his body.

Curious, Baby Pegasus floated closer to give the baby a sniff.

Hercules greeted the horse with a head butt. Startled, Pegasus whinnied and gave the baby a quick lick on the face.

Hercules giggled and threw his arms around his new friend.

Hera lifted her son from the crib and kissed him, then handed him to his father. "Mind the head," she instructed.

Zeus cradled his son in his arms. "He's so tiny," he whispered. "My boy—my little Hercules."

"How *sentimental*," a snide voice remarked.

Zeus frowned and looked up. He'd know that voice anywhere.

A tall bluish god with gray robes and hair of fire glided through the gathering.

Hades, Lord of the Underworld. Ruler of the Dead.

"You know," Hades joked, "I haven't been so choked up since I got a hunk of moussaka caught in my throat."

No one laughed.

Insulted, Hades frowned. "Is this an audience or a mosaic?"

"So, Hades, you finally made it. How are things in the Underworld?" Zeus asked.

"Just fine, you know? A little dark, a little gloomy. And, as always, full of dead people." Hades shrugged. "Whattaya gonna do?"

Hades stared down his nose at the baby. "Ah, there's the little sunspot. And here's a sucker for the little sucker." Like a dark magician, he pulled a skull pacifier from inside his robe and shoved it at the baby's mouth.

But instead of taking the gift, Hercules clutched the intruder's hand in a viselike grip. Hades winced and removed his throbbing hand. "Powerful little tyke ..."

"Come on, Hades," Zeus said, trying to make peace. "Don't be such a stiff. Join the celebration."

"Hey, love to, babe," Hades replied with a dramatic sigh. "But unlike you gods lounging about up here, I regrettably have a full-time gig—that you, by the way, Zeus, so charitably gave me. So can't. Love to, but can't." Leaving a faint wisp of smoke in the air, he swirled away.

"You ought to slow down," Zeus called after him. "You'll work yourself to death!" Suddenly the great god clutched his sides and bellowed with laughter. "Ha! Work yourself to death. Get it? Oh, brother, I *kill* myself!"

The gods and goddesses laughed at their ruler's wit.

CHAPTER II

Hades' home was the pits.

As in way, way down in the guts of the Earth, where bright light and fresh air gave way to darkness and despair.

Normally, upon returning to the Underworld, the smells of rotting spirits cheered him up a little.

But not today. After his visit to the ridiculously cheery world of Mount Olympus, Hades was in a black mood indeed.

As Charon the boatman paddled him across the river Styx, the hands of lost spirits rose from the dark waters, clutching at the sides of the boat. With a weary sigh, Hades flicked his fingers and zapped them with tiny hailstones of fire that sizzled in the murky water.

Soon they glided to the dock of his giant skull-like palace. Its windows stared blindly upon the world of the dead like empty eye sockets.

"Pain! Panic!" Hades barked out.

Two winged demons raced down the stairway. "Coming, master!"

But the pudgy red Pain tripped and fell down the stairs, landing at the bottom in a heap. As skinny blue Panic raced to help him, he stumbled and poked Pain in the backside with his pointed horns.

"Pain ..." Pain said painfully.

"And Panic ..." Panic moaned.

"Reporting for duty, sir!" they whimpered together.

Hades rolled his eyes. Ye gads, it was so hard to get good help these days, especially in *this* neighborhood. "Fine, fine. Just let me know the instant the Fates arrive."

"Oh, they're here!" Panic piped up.

"What!?" Hades roared. His hair ignited into a full mane of fire. "The Fates are *here*—and you didn't tell me?"

Pain and Panic fell to their knees, quaking in fear. "We are worms! Worthless worms!"

Poof! The demon twins morphed into slimy worms to demonstrate their utter regret.

"Memo to me," Hades muttered to himself as he stepped over them. "Maim these guys after my meeting."

Delighted not to have been smashed, Pain and Panic morphed back to their demon forms and trailed their master as he swept into his palace and down the hall to his favorite place:

The War Room.

Hades' eyes gleamed as he gazed upon his magnificent toy: a game board representing the cosmos. He had a game piece for everything: Mount Olympus, the planets, gods, monsters, humans.

Then he quickly turned his attention to the three hooded figures gathered together in the center of the room.

The Fates—Clotho, Lachesis, and Atropos. They were

powerful, indeed. For only *they* had the power to see the future.

The voices of the shriveled old hags crackled like dry leaves. Their wrinkled faces puckered around dark empty eye sockets. Above them floated a large round eyeball, which the three Fates shared. They tossed it between them and took turns plugging it into their own sockets.

These daughters of darkness spun the thread of life and held the fate of each living being in their bony hands.

Even now, someone's life hung by a thread.

Clotho had spun the thread. Lachesis had measured it out. And now Atropos picked up the scissors. "Darling," she rasped, "hold the Thread of Life good and tight."

Hades glanced at a sign above them: OVER 5,000,000,000 SERVED.

Atropos clipped the thread.

In the distance someone screamed.

"Incoming!" Clotho shouted.

A spirit flew out of a nearby chute and sailed through the room.

Hades checked the sign. The number flipped to 5,000,000,001.

Hades swept forward. "Ladies," he cooed in an overly sweet voice, "I'm so sorry that I'm—"

"Late!" they all said.

"We *knew* you would be," Lachesis said.

Hades laughed nervously. "Right, well, of course you'd know. You're the Fates!"

9

"We know *everything*," Clotho said.

"Past…" Lachesis hissed.

"Present…" Clotho added.

"And future!" Atropos finished. To the side, she whispered to Panic, "Indoor plumbing. It's going to be big!"

"Uh, great," Hades said politely. "Anyway, I was at a party, and I lost track of time."

"We *know*," Clotho said.

"Yeah, I *know* you know." Hades rolled his eyes. It was maddening to talk with someone who knew *all*! "Anyway. So here's the deal. Zeus—Mr. High and Mighty, Mr. 'Hey, You! Get Offa My Cloud'—now has a—"

"Bouncing baby brat," Clotho chimed in. "We *know*!"

"I know you know! I *know*! I get it!" Hades' hair flared. He gritted his teeth. Watch the temper, he warned himself. Deep breaths. Count to ten. Count to ten backward!

He mustn't upset the Fates, especially now.

For some time, Hades had been planning a coup—to overthrow Zeus and take over the universe. But now he was worried. And he needed all the help he could get.

Calm again, Hades raised his arm before him. Instantly a game piece that looked like baby Hercules appeared in the palm of his hand. "So let me just ask," he said timidly, holding the tiny figurine toward the Fates. "This Hercules … is this kid gonna mess up my hostile takeover bid or what? What do you think?"

Lachesis cackled and wagged a bony finger. "Oh, no, you don't! We're not supposed to reveal the future."

On the inside, Hades fumed. But on the outside, he smiled like a game show host in a toothpaste commercial. Maybe a little flattery would help. "Whoa, wait, time out. Can I ask you a question? Did you cut your hair? I mean, you look fabulous. You look like a Fate worse than death!"

Clotho giggled like a schoolgirl. She bent forward, and the eye fell out of her face—*plop*!—right into Pain's hands.

"Gross!" Pain squealed.

He tossed it like a hot potato into Panic's hands.

"Yeech! It's blinking!" Panic tossed it away and covered his own eyes.

Hades stooped to scoop it up, then handed it back to Clotho with a one hundred–watt smile. "Ladies, please. My fate is in your *lovely* hands."

The dried-up old witches rarely received such compliments. Actually they *never* received compliments.

This one worked like a charm.

"Oh, all right," Lachesis said.

Clotho tossed the eyeball into the air, where it floated above the three Fates' heads. They huddled beneath it as it began to swirl and glow. They were about to do what they did best.

They were about to tell the future.

"In eighteen years precisely," Clotho foretold, "the planets will align just so."

In the spinning eye Hades could see faint images of what the Fates could see.

"The time to act will be at hand," Lachesis said. "Unleash

the Titans."

"Hmm, good, good." Hades' eyes glowed with excitement.

"Then the once-proud Zeus will finally fall," Clotho chanted. "And you, Hades, will rule all!"

"Yes!" Hades cried, his fist pumping the air. "Hades rules!" He was so excited, he burst into flames.

But the Fates had not finished their prophecy.

Atropos raised a bony hand in warning: "A word of caution to this tale."

Hades frowned. "Excuse me?"

The Fates pointed to the floating eye once more. Now Hades could see a new image—a strong young man riding a winged horse.

"Should Hercules fight," Atropos warned, "you will fail."

Instantly the Fates disappeared. The image of Hercules as a grown man vanished like a wisp of smoke.

Hades' flames sputtered out.

It couldn't be!

So this baby with the rude manners was supposed to grow up into a muscle boy and threaten his entire future?

No way. Not if he could help it.

Hades swept down the hall till he came to a very special room. Inside, a single glass vial of potion floated in a pillar of fire.

Hades smiled at the brilliance of his plan. "Boys," he said to Pain and Panic, "here's a little riddle for you. How do you *kill* a god?"

"I do not know!" Pain announced confidently.

"Uh, you can't?" Panic guessed. "'Cause they're immortal?"

"Bingo!" Hades cried. "They're *immortal*."

Panic smiled hesitantly. Had he actually gotten something right for a change?

Hades reached for the vial of deep red liquid and held it up before his eyes. It glistened in the light from his flaming hair.

"So first," he murmured, "you gotta turn the little sunspot mortal…."

Morpheus, the god of sleep and dreams, draped the night sky with darkness.

In his heavenly nursery on Mount Olympus, baby Hercules smiled in his sleep. Pegasus snored softly nearby.

Dark shadows fell across the crib of the son of Zeus.

Zeus and Hera were sleeping peacefully on their king-size cloud.

Suddenly a noise startled them from their sleep.

Hera yawned and turned over. "What is it?" she mumbled.

Then she and her husband bolted upright in bed. "The baby!" they cried at once.

They rushed to the nursery, terrified of what they might find. Just inside, Pegasus poked his head out of a vase with a dazed look on his face.

Hera ran to the crib and reached for her son. Then she burst into tears.

"*Noooooooooo!*" Zeus's anguished roar shook Mount

13

Olympus and woke the gods and goddesses from their dreams.

Thunder and lightning pummeled the Earth.

The crib was empty.

Baby Hercules was gone.

CHAPTER III

"Now we did it!" Panic panicked. "Zeus is gonna use us for target practice!"

Panic and Pain dodged a wicked lightning bolt as they flew toward Earth.

Between them they clutched a giggling baby.

Hercules.

They'd slipped into the Mount Olympus nursery. Slam-dunked Pegasus in a Grecian urn. And kidnapped the baby right out from under Zeus's snoring nose.

Hades owed them big time for this one, they thought.

Moments later they crash-landed on Earth. It was raining cats and dogs, and they had to shout to be heard over the storm.

Zeus's angry thunderous roar shook the ground.

"Hurry," Panic cried. "Let's just kill the kid and get it over with, okay?"

"Listen, slo-mo," Pain fumed. "First, the brat has to drink the potion that'll turn him mortal."

"Then we kill him?" Panic guessed.

"Right!"

Pain pulled out a baby bottle filled with red liquid—the potion that Hades had given them. He slapped a nipple on it and stuffed it in the bawling baby's mouth.

"Here you go, kid," Pain said. "A little Grecian formula."

The baby's cries quieted as he hungrily drank.

As he swallowed the liquid, something strange happened. The godly glow that had surrounded him since birth began to fade.

"Wow—look at him!" Panic gasped. "He's *changing*! Can we kill him now?"

"No, no, no!" Pain said. "He has to drink the whole thing. *Every last drop.*"

Panic nervously wrung his hands. Hurry, hurry, he thought. Come on, kid. Just a little more.

"Who's there?" a man called out.

Startled, Pain and Panic panicked.

They fumbled the glass baby bottle, and it tumbled to the ground.

Panic winced.

Pain's hands flew to the ground.

But it was no use. The bottle had broken into dozens of glass shards. The last drop of potion soaked quickly into the wet ground.

Someone was coming!

The two winged demons ducked behind a nearby rock.

A tall human with a kindly face pushed aside the reeds. "Alcmene!" he called out. "Over here!"

The man's wife rushed over. As soon as she saw the baby, she scooped him up and cradled him in her arms. "Oh, you poor thing," she cooed.

Amphitryon glanced around in the pouring rain. "Is anybody there?" he called out.

Pain and Panic peeked out from behind their rock. Their faces lit up.

"Now?" Panic whispered.

"Now!" Pain whispered back.

Poof! Instantly the two demons transformed into deadly snakes. They slithered across the ground toward baby Hercules.

"Why, he must have been abandoned," Amphitryon said.

Alcmene's face glowed. For so many years she'd prayed to the gods to bless her with a child. But her prayers had gone unanswered. Now here was a child—a beautiful healthy boy—who needed someone to care for him. "Perhaps the gods have answered our prayers," she murmured.

"Perhaps they have." Amphitryon reached for the gold medallion hanging around the baby's neck. "Hercules," he read.

Just then the couple heard hissing behind them.

Poisonous snakes!

But before the snakes could strike, baby Hercules grabbed them and tied them in a knot, swung them like a lasso, and flung them into the night.

Amphitryon and Alcmene, stunned, stared at the baby.

Off in the distance, the two snakes crashed into a tree. Shrieking, they morphed back into their demon forms and tumbled to the ground.

"Oh, fab," Panic moaned. "Hades is gonna *kill* us when he

finds out!"

"You mean, *if* he finds out," Pain corrected.

"Of course he's gonna—" Panic stopped. "If? *If* is good."

The two demons exchanged a devilish grin.

Then, snickering, they hightailed it out of there. With any luck, they'd never see Hercules again.

Zeus searched heaven and earth. But by the time he found baby Hercules, it was too late.

His son had become mortal. And for all his great powers, there was nothing Zeus could do to change him back.

Zeus and Hera wept great cloudbursts of tears.

Hercules could never come home.

CHAPTER IV

Eighteen years later ...

"Hercules! Slow down!"

Amphitryon hung on to the sides of his barley cart as it rumbled rapidly toward the marketplace.

Amphitryon was now a white-haired old man. His donkey Penelope, her leg bandaged, sat beside him in the cart.

Pulling the cart instead was a handsome but awkward teenager—his adopted son, Hercules.

The boy had grown up in an ordinary family. But though he was mortal, he was far from ordinary.

Because he did not drink that very last drop of Hades' potion, he lost all his powers but one: his great strength.

Hercules ran beneath the arch that led to the marketplace. But the cart struck the two columns and nearly knocked them down.

"Watch where you're going!" a workman yelled from the top.

"Oops! Sorry." Hercules stopped in front of a shop.

"Thanks, son," Amphitryon said as he climbed down from the cart. "Now, Hercules, this time, please just—"

"I know, I know, Pop. Stay by the cart."

"That's my boy." Amphitryon hurried off.

But Hercules was restless. The marketplace was filled with the sights and smells and sounds of adventure. There was so much to see and do and buy. It was boring just to stand around.

Across the way he saw Demetrius, the potter, struggling to place a heavy vase on a high shelf.

"Here, let me help you with that," Hercules offered.

The man's eyes flew open. "No—no! I've got it! I'm fine! Y—you just run along."

"You sure?" Hercules asked, puzzled.

"Oh, yes! Absolutely. Go on, now. Thanks."

Hercules shrugged and wandered down the street.

Whoosh!

A discus landed at his feet, and Hercules brightened. He glanced up at some teenage boys staring at him from down the street. "Hey, you need an extra guy?" he asked hopefully.

The boys glanced nervously at one another. Nobody wanted to play with Hercules. It was too dangerous! Besides, he was weird.

"Uh, sorry, Herc!" said a boy named Ithicles. "We already got five. And we want to keep it an even number."

"But—"

"What a geek!" one of the boys snickered.

"Maybe we should just call him Jerk-ules!" another joked.

Hercules overheard their cruel remarks, and his shoulders sagged.

A few minutes later he heard Ithicles shout, "Heads up!"

The discus was heading his way again. Maybe if he showed them how well he could catch . . . "I got it!" he cried.

"No," Ithicles shouted. "Stop!"

Using the strength of his powerful legs, Hercules leaped thirty feet in the air and caught the discus. But he had no control.

Coming down he smashed into a giant stone pillar just as Amphitryon stepped out into the street.

"Watch out!" Hercules hollered.

Villagers dived for cover as one column struck another column, which struck another column. . . . Like giant dominoes, the columns tumbled down until the entire colonnade collapsed. Chickens flew their broken coops. Jugs and jars smashed to the ground. Fresh vegetables and other goods spilled into the dirt.

Hercules rushed to help, but slipped in a puddle of spilled olive oil. With a yelp, he slid smack into Demetrius's shelves of fragile pottery and crashed into Demetrius.

When the dust settled, Hercules stood in the middle of all the rubble. Blushing, he reached down and picked up the discus.

Ithicles snatched it from his hands. "Nice catch," he said sarcastically.

Hercules stared at the ground.

"This is the last straw!" Demetrius said.

"That boy is a menace!" a woman called out.

"He's too dangerous to be around *normal* people!" one of the workmen complained.

21

Amphitryon held up his hands. "He didn't mean any harm. He's just a kid. He can't control his strength."

"I'm warning you," Demetrius said angrily as he picked up his broken pottery. "You keep that—that freak away from here!"

The crowd began to shout and jeer.

"Freak!"

"Go away!"

It took all of Hercules' strength to hold back the tears.

Amphitryon steered his son toward their cart. "Come on, Son. Let's go home."

That evening Amphitryon sat with Hercules on the hillside of their olive grove, watching the sun dip low in the sky. "Son, you shouldn't let those things they said back there get to you."

"But, Pop, they're right," Hercules said. "I *am* a freak! I'm not *like* other people." Idly he picked up a thick olive branch and broke it in two. It snapped like a toothpick. "I try to fit in. I really do. I just *can't*!"

Hercules stared out across the valley. How could he explain? "Sometimes I feel like . . . like I really don't belong here. Like I'm supposed to be someplace *else*. Like I—"

"Son—"

"I know it doesn't make any sense." Hercules stood up and strode away from his father. He didn't know where he was going, but he needed to take a walk. He needed to be alone.

Wisely, his father let him go.

Hercules had often dreamed of a far-off place where he wouldn't be the geek. Where crowds would *cheer* when they saw him—instead of running in the opposite direction.

Sometimes he felt like hitting the road to search for that place. He'd go the distance, walk every mile without complaining.

He'd go almost anywhere to feel that he belonged.

Hercules searched the sky as if he might find the answer somewhere among the clouds.

But all it told him was that the sun was setting, and there were still chores to be done back at the farm. With a sigh, Hercules turned around and walked back home.

His mother and father stood in the doorway, waiting for him with strange looks on their faces.

"Hercules," his father began. "There's something your mother and I have been meaning to tell you...."

CHAPTER V

The news blew him away.

Hercules loved Amphitryon and Alcmene with all his heart and had always tried to be a good son to them.

Oh, sometimes, late at night, he had wondered why he didn't have any brothers or sisters or why he didn't look much like his mother or father. And why was he so darn strong?

Now his parents had finally told him why.

He was adopted.

"But if you found me," Hercules said, "then where did I come from? Why was I left here?"

Alcmene lifted a small parcel from her lap. Slowly she unwrapped a shining gold medallion.

"This was around your neck when we found you," she said. With reverence, she whispered, "It's the symbol of the gods."

Hercules took the shining medallion in his hands. Here was a clue to all his questions!

"This is it!" he exclaimed excitedly. "Don't you see? Maybe *they* have the answers. I'll go to the Temple of Zeus and—"

He broke off when he saw the pain on his parents' faces.

Hercules shoved a hand through his hair. This was not going to be easy. "Ma, Pop, you're the greatest parents anyone could have. But I gotta know." His eyes begged them to understand.

His parents smiled through their tears.

They loved him enough to let him go.

At dawn the next morning Hercules took a good long look at the farm he'd always known as home. Who knew when—or if—he'd ever be back?

Alcmene's eyes brimmed with tears as she draped a cloak around her son's shoulders and kissed his cheek. He and Amphitryon embraced. Then Hercules tossed his rucksack over his shoulder and walked eagerly down the road.

He was on his way to finding out who he was.

His travels took him to the great Temple of Zeus. Reverently he entered.

Inside, a giant statue of Zeus towered above him. Hercules gasped. The statue wore a medallion just like his!

Hercules dropped his rucksack and knelt. "Oh, mighty Zeus, please, hear me and answer my prayer. I need to know: Who am I? Where do I belong?"

A clap of thunder and a flash of lightning made him jump.

And then the giant statue of Zeus came to life!

Hercules stared. His jaw dropped.

And then the statue *spoke*. "My boy. My little Hercules."

Hercules screamed and scuttled backward toward the door.

"Hey, hold on, kiddo!" Zeus said. "What's your hurry?" He

picked up Hercules in his massive hands. Hercules felt like an insect as he tried to escape the great god's enormous fingers.

"After all these years, is this the kind of hello you give to your father?"

Hercules froze. "F-f-father?"

"Didn't know you had a famous father, did you?" Zeus said merrily. "Surprise!" He smiled lovingly at his son. "Look how much you've grown. Why, you've got your mother's beautiful eyes . . . and my strong chin."

"B-but if you're my father," Hercules sputtered, "that would make me a . . ."

Zeus nodded. "A god."

"A god?" Hercules said. "A *god*! I—I don't understand."

"Hey, you wanted answers," Zeus said, "and by thunder, you're old enough to know the truth!"

Hercules felt dizzy. He sat on Zeus's palm and took a deep breath. "But why did you leave me on Earth? Didn't you want me?"

"Of course we did!" Zeus responded in anguish. "Your mother and I loved you with all our hearts. But someone stole you from us and turned you mortal." Gently he added, "And only gods can live on Mount Olympus."

Hercules rubbed his face. Wow—so he was a god. Except he wasn't anymore. "You mean, you can't do anything about it?"

"*I* can't, Hercules," Zeus replied.

Hercules' heart sank.

"But *you* can," Zeus added.

"Really? What? I'll do *anything*!"

Zeus's laughter rumbled through the temple. "That's *exactly* what your old man wanted to hear." Then his face turned very serious. "Hercules, if you can prove yourself a *true hero* on Earth, your godhood will be restored."

"A true hero … Great!" he exclaimed. Then he frowned. "Uh, exactly how do you become a true hero?"

"First, you must seek out Philoctetes, the trainer of heroes," Zeus explained. "But that's not all. Then—"

"I can do it!" Hercules interrupted. "I know I can. Whoo!"

Hercules ran for the door.

Zeus grabbed him by the tunic and yanked him back. "Whoa! Hold your horses. Which reminds me …" He put his fingers to his lips and let out an ear-shattering whistle.

Seconds later a full-grown horse flew into the temple.

"You probably don't remember him," Zeus said. "But you two go way back, Son."

Cool horse, Hercules thought. But he shook his head. He couldn't remember ever seeing any horse with *wings*.

Pegasus gave Hercules the same sloppy lick he'd given him as a baby. Then he gave him a head butt.

Suddenly Hercules smiled. He remembered! "Pegasus!"

The horse grinned and whinnied.

"I'll find Philoctetes," Hercules told his father as he climbed onto Pegasus's back. "And become a true hero!"

"That's the spirit!" Zeus cried.

Hercules waved. "I won't let you down, Father."

Then Zeus puffed out his cheeks and *bleeeeeeew!*
The wind launched Hercules and Pegasus into the sky.
"Yeeee-ha!" Hercules cried.
Zeus dashed a stray tear from his eye. "Good luck, Son!"

Off in the cosmos the celestial timer was ticking. The alignment of the planets foretold by the Fates seventeen years ago was drawing close.

CHAPTER VI

Hercules and Pegasus banked into a turn. Together they descended through the morning mist and landed on the island of Idra.

The place was a wreck.

The grass was overgrown. Remnants of broken statues littered the ground.

Hercules frowned. "You *sure* this is the right place?"

Pegasus nodded.

Just then Hercules heard frantic bleating. He noticed the rear end of a goat sticking out of the bushes. "What's the matter, little guy? You stuck?"

But when he pulled him out, he was in for a shock.

The bottom half of the creature looked like a goat. But the top half looked like a fat little man with horns.

Hercules' jaw dropped.

"What's the matter?" the goat-man snapped. "Ya never seen a satyr before?"

"Uh, no," Hercules replied. He cleared his throat, then asked, "Can you help us? We're looking for someone called Philoctetes."

The little goat-man sighed. "Just call me Phil."

Delighted, Hercules grabbed his hand and shook.

29

"Yow!" the goat-man yelped.

"Boy, am I glad to meet you! I'm Hercules, and I need your help. I want to become a hero—a true hero!"

"Sorry, kid. Can't help you." Phil trotted back into his hut and slammed the door.

"Wait!" Hercules grabbed the doorknob and yanked hard. The whole door came off its hinges—with Phil still holding the door. "Sorry," Hercules mumbled. "Uh, why not?"

"Two words," Phil answered. "I … am … retired."

Herc counted the words, confused, then shook his head. "Look, I gotta do this. Haven't you ever had a dream? Something you wanted so bad you'd do anything?"

Phil stared at Hercules a moment, measuring his worth. "Kid, come inside. I wanna show you something."

Hercules had to duck his head as he followed Phil. Inside he looked around in awe. The place was like a sports museum! It was filled with swords, shields, paintings, and sculptures of some of the greatest heroes the world had ever known.

"I trained all these would-be heroes," Phil said. "And every single one of those bums let me down. None of 'em could go the distance."

He pointed to a statue. Hercules knew this guy—Achilles, the greatest Greek warrior in the Trojan War. When he was a baby, Achilles' mother dipped him in a magical river, hoping to make him immortal. But she missed the spot where she held him by his heel. And that was where he remained mortal.

"Achilles. Now, there's a guy who had it all," Phil said. "The build, the foot speed. He could jab! He could take a hit! He could keep on coming! But that heel of his!" He gave the heel of the statue a tiny flick with his finger.

Crash! The whole statue crumbled to the floor.

"He barely gets nicked there once and *kaboom*! He's history!"

Phil wandered over to his desk and picked up a scroll. "Yeah, I had a dream once. I dreamed I was gonna train the greatest hero there ever was. So great, the gods would hang a picture of him in the stars."

He unrolled the scroll. Hercules admired the picture of a heroic figure as a constellation.

"And people would say, 'That's Phil's boy.'" He angrily rolled the scroll back up. "Ah, but dreams are for rookies. A guy can only take so much disappointment."

"But I'm different from those other guys, Phil!" Hercules pleaded. "I can *do* this! I can *go* the distance. Come on, I'll show you!" He grabbed Phil's arm and dragged him out the door.

"You don't give up, do you?" Phil muttered.

Outside Hercules raised the gigantic stone arm and shield of a broken statue above his head. Then he heaved it into the sea as if it were a small pebble.

Phil was impressed. "Wow! You know, maybe if—" Then he stopped himself. "No, snap out of it. I'm too old to get mixed up in this stuff again." He started to walk away.

"But if I don't become a true hero," Hercules said, "I'll never be able to rejoin my father, Zeus."

Phil screeched to a halt. "Hold it! *Zeus* is your father? Zeus, the big guy? Mr. Lightning Bolts?"

"It's the truth," Hercules insisted.

"Please!" Phil threw up his hands and jumped onto a tree stump. "So you want to be a hero? Well, I've been around the block before with kids like you, and each and every one was a huge disappointment! So even though a kid of Zeus is asking me, my answer is two words—"

"*Zap!* A quick comment from Zeus in the form of a lightning bolt crashed at Phil's feet.

So he ditched the two words he was going to say, and picked two that were slightly more politically correct: "All right."

"You mean you'll do it?" Hercules exclaimed. "You won't be sorry! So when do we start? Can we start now? Huh? Huh?"

Phil grabbed his head in his hands. "*Oy vay!* There goes my ulcer!"

With a sigh, he hurried inside his hut to drag all his hero-training gear out of mothballs.

I must be crazy . . . , he thought.

But Hercules threw himself into his training.

He did push-ups, pull-ups, sit-ups, and jumping jacks. He jumped rope, leaped over hurdles, and lifted weights. He ran track and did step aerobics. Every day, all day, no excuses.

"Rule number seventeen," Phil lectured. "When rescuing a damsel in distress, always handle with care!"

Phweeeet! He blew his whistle, and Hercules charged

away. He grabbed the dummy damsel. He carried her onto the log bridge. This was easy!

But then he tripped and split the log with his head. He landed in the creek, and the dummy damsel lost her head.

Phil groaned. "Rule number ninety-five, kid: concentrate!"

Pegasus tossed a bunch of swords to Hercules. He threw them and pinned Phil to a tree.

"Rule number ninety-six," Phil said. *"Aim!"*

Gradually, after weeks and weeks of hard training, Hercules grew stronger and gained more control of his strength.

Finally the day came.

Hercules slapped Pegasus a high five. "Next stop—Olympus!"

"Just take it easy, champ," Phil warned him.

"I am ready!" Hercules exclaimed. "I want to get off this island. I wanna battle some monsters, rescue some real damsels. You know, heroic stuff. Aw, come on, Phil."

"Well, okay, okay. You want a road test? Saddle up, kid. We're going to Thebes."

CHAPTER VII

"Eeeeeeeeeek!"

Hercules and Phil soared through the clouds on Pegasus. Down below, someone was screaming.

It looked as if they wouldn't have to wait to get to Thebes to find trouble.

"Sounds like your basic D.I.D.," Phil said. "Damsel in Distress." He hung on as Pegasus dived for the ground.

Moments later they peered through some thick trees, trying to find the damsel who needed help.

Over there! A very beautiful young damsel was being chased by a very *ugly* centaur—a creature with the head and upper body of a man and the body of a horse. "Not so fast, sweetheart!" he cackled as he grabbed the young woman.

"Nessus!" she screamed. "Put me down!"

"Now, remember, kid," Phil whispered to Hercules. "*Analyze* the situation. Don't just barrel in without thinking and—"

But Hercules had already barreled in. "Halt!" he ordered.

Nessus and the girl stopped struggling.

"Step aside, two-legs!" Nessus growled.

Hmmm. Maybe good manners would work better. "Pardon me, my good sir. I'll have to ask you to release the

34

young lady."

"Back off, Atlas," the young lady snapped.

Hercules was stunned. "But aren't you a damsel in distress?"

"I'm a damsel. I'm in distress. But I can handle it." She shot him a fake smile. "Have a nice day."

Hercules scratched his head. None of his hero workshops had said what to do if the damsel didn't *want* to be rescued. "Uh, ma'am, I'm afraid you may not realize—"

Wham! Nessus very rudely punched Hercules in the jaw.

Hercules splashed into the river and came up sputtering.

"What are you doing?" Phil hollered. "Get your sword!"

Hercules wiped the water from his face and frantically searched the water. "Right, rule number fifteen: a hero is only as good as his weapon." With a smile he aimed his—

Fish.

Nessus roared with laughter. Then *blam!* With the next punch Hercules rammed headfirst into a rock jutting out of the water.

Pegasus snorted angrily and started forward, but Phil held him back. "Whoa, hold it. He's gotta do it on his own. Come on, kid!" he shouted at Hercules. "Concentrate! Use your head!"

"Oh." Hercules nodded. Then he lowered his head like a battering ram and plowed into the huge centaur's gut.

"All right!" Phil cheered. "Not bad!" To himself he mumbled, "Not exactly what I had in mind, but not bad."

When Hercules hit Nessus, the ugly centaur stumbled

and lost his grip on the girl. With a shriek, she splashed into the river.

"Aw, gee, Miss," Hercules said. He picked her up and set her down next to Phil. "I'm really sorry. That was dumb!"

The girl just glared and wrung out her long auburn hair.

But there was no time for chitchat—Nessus was charging. "Excuse me," he said politely, then dashed back into the fight.

Hercules struggled with the centaur. Then he pulled a lucky punch that knocked Nessus out of his horseshoes and sent him zooming into the sky.

When the centaur crashed back into the water, he sat up gasping for air. He had a huge lump on his bald head. One by one, the horseshoes clunked him on the head. A ringer!

"How was that, Phil?" Hercules asked.

Phil shook his head. "You can get away with mistakes like those in the minor decathlons, but this is the big leagues."

"At least I beat him, didn't I?" Hercules asked.

"Next time," Phil said, "don't let your guard down because of a pair of big goo-goo eyes. It's like I keep telling you—you gotta stay focused and—"

Hercules was focused. Focused on the beautiful damsel he'd just rescued. He walked toward Pegasus, and the horse held up a hoof for a high five.

Glassy-eyed, Hercules walked right past him.

"Are you all right, Miss, uh ..."

"Megara," she said. "My friends call me Meg. At least they would, if I had any friends," she muttered. "So, did they give you a name along with all those rippling muscles?"

"Hercules. My name is Hercules."

"Well, thanks for everything, Herc. It's been a real slice."

"Wait!" Hercules said. "Um, can we give you a ride?"

Pegasus didn't like that one bit. He gave an angry snort and flew up into an apple tree.

"I don't think your pinto likes me very much," Meg said.

"Pegasus? Oh, no, don't be silly. He'd be happy to—"

Bonk! Pegasus beaned Hercules with an apple from the tree.

"Ow!"

Meg grinned. "It'll be all right. I'm a big tough girl. Bye-bye, Wonder Boy."

Hercules watched her until she disappeared down the road. "She's something, isn't she, Phil?"

"Oh, yeah, she's really something," Phil said sarcastically. "A real *pain*." He stared at his friend's lovesick face and sighed. "Come on, Herc. We got a job to do, remember?"

But all Herc could remember were those beautiful eyes.

Down the road Meg's smile faded as her rescuers flew away. A weird shiver ran through her. She stopped and looked around.

Just ahead, a bunny and a gopher sat in the middle of the road and twitched their little noses at her.

"Swell. Just what I needed," she said, with her hands on her hips. "A couple of rodents looking for a theme park."

"Who are you calling a rodent, sister?" the bunny snapped.

"I'm a bunny."

"And I'm his gopher!" the other one insisted.

Meg folded her arms and nodded. "I thought I smelled a rat!"

Poof!

The woodland creatures morphed into Pain and Panic.

Meg wrinkled her nose as a smoky smelling arm seemed to reach out from nowhere and grab her by the wrist.

Hades. Her least favorite person in the world. Or rather, Underworld. "Speak of the devil ..."

"Meg, my little flower, my little bird, my little Nut-Meg." Hades smiled at her, then pretended to pout. "What exactly happened here? I thought you were going to persuade the River Guardian to join my team for the uprising against Zeus."

Meg shrugged. "I gave it my best shot."

Hades smiled a cold hard smile. "Fine. Instead of *subtracting* two years from your sentence—hey! I'm going to add two *on*. Okay? Give *that* your best shot."

"Look, it wasn't my fault!" Meg protested. "This Wonder Boy—this Hercules—muscled his way in."

Hades froze. His eyes narrowed. "*What* was that name again?"

"Hercules."

Hades groaned.

"He comes on to me with this big innocent farmboy routine," Meg explained. "But I saw through that in a minute."

"Wait a minute," Pain said, thinking hard. "Wasn't *Hercules* the name of that kid we were supposed to ki—"

Hades grabbed the little demons by their tails.

"Run for it!" Panic shrieked.

"Mommy!" Pain cried.

"So you took care of him, hmmm?" Hades demanded. "'Dead as a doornail.' Weren't those your exact words?"

"Uh, this might be a different Hercules?" Pain suggested.

"Yeah," Panic agreed. "You know, Hercules is a very popular name nowadays."

Hades threw the demons against the wall. They morphed into tiny roaches to prove how worthless they were.

Hades paced the forest floor. "I'm about to rearrange the cosmos. And the one jerk who can louse it up is waltzing around in the woods!?" His anger was so hot, it burned down trees.

"Wait!" Pain begged as he and Panic morphed back into their regular selves. "We can still cut in on his waltzing, big guy."

"That's right," Panic agreed. "At least we turned him into a mortal." He glanced at Pain. "Didn't we?"

Hades' rage died down to a smolder. He drew Pain, Panic, and Meg into his smoky embrace. "Fortunately for the three of you, we still have time to correct this little oversight.

"And *this* time, no foul-ups!"

CHAPTER VIII

"Wow! Is this all one town?" Hercules exclaimed.

"One town, a million troubles," Phil said as they made their way down the crowded street. "The one and only city of Thebes. Stick with me," he warned. "The city is a dangerous place."

A taxi chariot tore down the avenue and nearly ran them down. "Look where yer goin', numbskull!" the cabdriver yelled.

"Hey, I'm walking here!" Phil shouted back. "See what I mean?" he asked Hercules. "I'm telling ya—wackos!"

Hercules' eyes were as big as saucers as they walked around town. There were vendors selling pita bread. Shady-looking guys trying to sell hot sundials. And more people than he'd ever seen in his entire life.

A man with wild hair and crazed eyes ran up to Hercules and grabbed him by his cape. "The end is coming! Can't you feel it?"

Phil shoved the man aside. "Yeah, yeah. Thank you for that info." To Hercules, he whispered, "Just stare at the sidewalk. Don't make eye contact. People here are nuts. That's because they live in a city of turmoil. Trust me, kid. You're gonna be just what the doctor ordered."

As they came to the town square, they saw a crowd of people gathered round the fountain. Hercules noticed that everyone looked extremely depressed.

"It was tragic," he heard a lumpy woman tell her neighbors. "We lost *everything* in the fire."

"Now, were the fires before or after the earthquake?" a fat man asked, trying to remember.

"After," a thin woman said firmly. "I remember."

"But before the flood," the lumpy woman added.

An old man shook his head. "Don't even get me started on the crime rate!"

"Thebes has certainly gone downhill in a hurry," the lumpy woman sorrowfully agreed.

Shyly Hercules approached the crowd. "Excuse me . . ."

The people stopped talking and stared at him suspiciously.

Hercules felt a blush creep up his neck, but he plunged ahead. "It, uh, seems to me that what you folks need is a hero."

The people gave him blank looks.

"Yeah?" the fat man asked skeptically. "And who are you?"

"I'm Hercules. And, uh, I happen to be a hero."

The fat man laughed. The lumpy woman snickered.

"Is that so?" the old man asked. "Ever saved a town before?"

"No, not exactly—"

"Ever reversed a natural disaster?" the fat man asked.

"Well, uh, no . . ."

"Aw, listen to him—he's just another chariot chaser." The

fat man rolled his eyes. "This we need!"

The crowd started to shuffle off.

"Don't you pea-brains get it?" Phil hollered at them. "This kid is the genuine article."

"Hey!" said a man with singed hair. "Isn't that the goat-man who trained Achilles?"

Phil shot him a warning look. "Watch it, pal."

"Yeah, you're right!" the fat man agreed. "Hey, nice job on those heels! Ya missed a spot!"

Phil jumped the guy and wrestled him to the ground. Hercules had to drag him off.

"Young man," the fat woman told Hercules. "We need a *professional* hero. Not an amateur."

She and the others turned their backs on Hercules and melted into the crowds.

"Wait! Stop!" Hercules called out.

But no one listened. The crowds swirled past him as if he were a tiny pebble in a river.

Hercules sighed. "How am I supposed to prove myself if nobody will give me a chance?"

"You'll get your chance," Phil assured him. "You just need some kind of catastrophe or disaster."

Suddenly they heard a commotion. Hercules looked up and saw the beautiful girl from the forest running toward him.

Phil rolled his eyes. "Speaking of disasters . . ."

"Help!" she cried. "There's been a terrible accident!"

"Meg?" Hercules asked.

"Wonder Boy!" Meg exclaimed. "Thank goodness!"

"What's wrong?"

Meg grasped his arm, gasping for breath. "Outside of town ... two little boys ... They're trapped in a rock slide!"

Hercules' eyes glowed. "Phil, this is *great*!"

Meg frowned. "You're really choked up about this, aren't you?"

"Come on!" He hauled her onto Pegasus.

"No!" Meg squealed. "I have this terrible fear of—"

Pegasus soared into the sky.

"H-E-I-G-H-T-S!" Petrified, Meg closed her eyes and dug her fingernails into Hercules' shoulders.

Pegasus whinnied. He enjoyed making her stomach turn.

CHAPTER IX

At the outskirts of town, Pegasus made a perfect landing in a rocky gorge. A crowd had gathered at the scene of the accident. The two boys lay trapped beneath a giant rock.

"Help!" one boy hollered.

"We're suffocating!" the other boy cried.

"Somebody call IX-I-I!" the first boy screamed.

Hercules rushed to their side. "Easy, fellas, you'll be all right." With a grunt, he lifted the rock. The boys were free!

Meg was amazed. But the townsfolk only clapped politely.

"Jeepers, mister," the first boy said. "You're strong!"

Hercules smiled and patted them on their heads. "Well, just try to be a little more careful next time, okay, kids?"

"We sure will," the first boy said with a smile.

With a wave the two boys ran off up the hill. Away from the crowd. Behind a big rock.

Hades was waiting for them.

The Lord of the Dead smiled at the two boys as he snacked on a bowlful of worms. Disasters always made him hungry. "Stirring performance, boys. I was really moved."

The boys grinned as they morphed into Pain and Panic.

Hades smacked his lips and wiped his mouth on his sleeve. "And hey, two thumbs up for our leading lady, Meg."

He raised his fists—and his thumbs lit up like candles.

Down below Meg felt someone's eyes burn into her back. She glanced up the hill at Hades. Then she turned back to Hercules with a guilty look on her face. "Get out of here, you big lug," she whispered, "while you still can."

"I did great!" Hercules cried to Phil. "They even applauded! Sort of."

Phil was just about to congratulate him when a high-pitched hissing sound echoed along the canyon walls.

"I hate to burst your bubble, kid. But that ain't applause," said Phil.

The hissing grew louder and louder. Lightning flashed as a creature poked its head from the inky depths of a cave in the mountainside. It was a giant serpentlike monster with scaly skin and sharp fangs.

"Phil," Hercules gasped, "wh-what do you call that thing?"

Phil took cover. "Two words: Run for it!"

"The Hydra!" screamed a woman in the crowd.

High above them Hades smiled. "Let's get ready to rumble!"

The monster lunged at Hercules, but he tumbled away and drew his sword. Jumping to his feet, he used all the skills Phil had taught him to dodge the serpent and keep her at bay.

"That's it," Phil coached from behind the rock. "Dance around him! Watch the teeth! Keep moving! Come on, lead with your left, lead with your *left*—"

Hercules struck out with his right. The serpent struck

him and sent him flying.

Phil rolled his eyes, exasperated. "Your *other* left!"

Hercules landed hard on the rocky ground. Quickly he rolled to his feet and faced the Hydra.

The Hydra lashed out with her tongue and caught Hercules by the ankle. She flipped him in the air and—

Gulp! She swallowed Hercules whole—then let out a huge, satisfied *burp!* The Hydra smiled.

But then her eyes crossed. A sick look spread across her face. A man-sized bulge formed in her throat.

With a roar, Hercules slashed his way out of the monster's throat. The huge head tore from the body and flew into the air, then landed in the middle of the crowd.

Hercules stood on the neck of the beheaded monster. For a moment her body still stood there, trembling. Then, with a shudder, it crashed to the ground.

This time the crowd clapped with more enthusiasm.

"All right!" Phil shouted as he rushed up to his student.

"See, Phil," Hercules gasped, swaying a little on his feet. "That . . . that wasn't so hard . . ."

But suddenly an eerie *hissssss* wheezed from the wound in the Hydra's neck.

"That doesn't sound good," Phil muttered.

With prickles dancing down their spines, they slowly turned.

Three—count 'em—THREE separate writhing heads oozed from the wound, ready to strike.

Hercules whistled sharply through his teeth, and Pegasus

flew to his side. Together they soared into the sky.

With a mighty blow, Hercules sliced off one of the heads. But before he could attack another, six more grew in its place.

Frantically Hercules sliced off another head.

Twelve more heads gushed out to replace it!

Faster and faster, Hercules chopped at the hideous monster.

Soon the monster had *thirty* heads.

"Will you forget the head-slicing thing?" Phil yelled. "It ain't working!"

Suddenly one of the heads struck Hercules, and he fell— right into the hissing swarm of heads.

"Ewwwwww!" the crowd squealed.

The Hydra wrapped her neck around Hercules, squeezing him like a boa constrictor. Four hissing heads dived for him.

At the last second Hercules slipped down in the coil.

One monster head bit into the neck of another.

As that neck uncoiled in pain, it flung Hercules high into the air. Hercules landed on the side of a cliff. The rock tore his skin as he desperately fought for a fingerhold.

Hades had been watching every second of the battle. Now he leaned forward as a shiver of anticipation ran through him. "My favorite part of the game," he hissed. *"Sudden death!"*

Just as Hercules managed a good grip on the cliff, he felt himself pinned to the rock by the sharp talon of the Hydra's foot. He turned to face his attacker, and his heart sank.

All thirty heads of the monster stared at him, licking

their slimy lips, ready for the final attack.

Thunder and lightning shook the canyon.

And Hercules, at the very last second, had an idea.

As all thirty heads lunged at him at once, Hercules smashed his powerful fists as hard as he could into the mountainside. The blow shook the mountain to its core—and triggered an avalanche.

With an ear-splitting rumble, the entire mountainside seemed to collapse, burying the Hydra in rock.

For a moment no one in the crowd moved—or even breathed.

They waited as the dust settled.

But there was no sign of Hercules.

Meg's hands flew to her mouth.

Pegasus whinnied mournfully.

Phil stared sadly at his hooves. "There goes another one. Just like Achilles . . ."

The mighty hero Hercules had defeated the Hydra.

But now he lay buried in a rocky grave.

CHAPTER X

Meg stared sorrowfully at the pile of rubble.

She was Hades' slave. She *had* to do what he told her. Didn't she?

That didn't help much as she mourned her role in the death of an innocent young hero.

Poor Wonder Boy, she thought. He was a good kid.

Hades giggled. "Game, set, match!" He pulled out a cigar and lit it—with his flaming finger.

Meg bit her tongue to hold back the nasty remarks that came to mind. If the creep didn't own her soul, why, she'd—

A faint sound from the mountainside stole her attention.

A few rocks began to tumble from the pile.

Was the Hydra still alive?

The crowd drew back in fear.

The Hydra's talon uncurled. And then—

Something crawled out of the rubble.

"Hercules!" Meg gasped.

The crowd stared in shock for a moment, then burst into wild cheers. Why, this kid—this country hick from nowhere—was the genuine article. A *real* hero!

Shouting and cheering, the people rushed forward and raised him to their shoulders.

Hercules beamed. "Hey, Phil," he called out. "Even you gotta admit—that was pretty heroic!"

Phil ran up on top of the pile of boulders and yelled back, "Ya did it! You won by a landslide!"

The canyon echoed with the sounds of cheers and celebration.

Up in the bleachers of the losing team, Hades seethed. His cigar burned up into ashes. In fury, he crushed the nearest thing he could lay his hands on.

The heads of Pain and Panic.

"Hades . . . mad!" Pain managed to gasp.

"Well, whaddya know," Meg whispered, shaking her head in admiration. This was the first time she'd ever seen anyone play against Hades—and win.

From that day forward Hercules could do no wrong. He was so hot, steam looked cool.

Over the next few weeks, Hades tried everything. He sent legions of monsters to take Hercules down. A giant boar. Harpies. Even a sea monster.

One by one, Hercules destroyed them.

The people in the city of Thebes adored him. They unveiled a giant statue of him in the town square. He was number one in every Greek opinion poll.

He and Pegasus even got their hand and footprints—and hoofprints—in cement in the sidewalk before the Amphitheater with all the other celebrities.

Soon merchants in the marketplace were cashing in on

his fame. They sold athletic sandals and clothes with Hercules' picture on them.

Moms and dads fought to buy their kids Hercules action figures, which quickly sold out.

It didn't matter what it was—vases, lunch boxes, fast food, toys—if it had Hercules' name on it, it sold like hotcakes.

When he wasn't slaying monsters, Hercules kept busy speaking at schools, garden clubs, and conferences.

What with the appearance fees and royalties from all the licensed products, Hercules grew rich.

It was a dream come true. Overnight he went from the town's biggest zero to the town's biggest hero.

Off on the hillside, Pain and Panic held a large vase between them. A picture of Hercules was painted on the side.

"Pull!" Hades shouted.

Pain and Panic tossed the vase into the sky.

Smoldering in anger, Hades took careful aim. Then he zapped the priceless vase with a ball of fire from his fingertips.

Pain and Panic ducked as pottery shards rained down on them.

"Nice shooting," Meg said dryly.

Hades swirled around. "I can't *believe* this guy! I throw everything I've got at him, and he doesn't even—"

Hades stopped midsentence and glared at Pain's feet. "What are *those*?"

Pain took a nervous step backward, wishing his feet

would sink into the earth. "Um, I dunno," he hedged. He glanced down at his sandals—his Herc-Air sandals. "Um, I thought they looked kind of dashing," he mumbled.

Hades did a slow burn. "I've got twenty-four hours to get rid of this bozo," he growled, "or the entire scheme I've been setting up for *eighteen* years goes up in smoke! *And you're wearing his merchandise!!!*"

Hades lunged for Pain's throat when a weird slurping sound made him stop. He whirled around.

Panic was slurping nectar from his new Hercules sports cup.

"Uh, thirsty?" Panic asked nervously, holding up the cup.

Hades exploded. Pain and Panic were singed from head to toe.

Meg snickered. "Looks like your game's over," she commented. "Wonder Boy's hitting every curve you throw at him."

Hades glared at her. But then, slowly, his sneer curled up into a wicked smile. "Maybe I haven't been throwing the *right* curves at him, Meg, my sweet—"

Uh-oh. She knew what he was thinking. "Don't even go there."

Hades circled Meg, looking her up and down. "See, he's gotta have a weakness. Because everybody's got a weakness. I mean, for Pandora, it was the box thing. For the Trojans, hey, they bet on the wrong horse. We simply need to find Wonder Boy's weakness."

"Get your little imps to handle it," Meg said coldly.

Hades chuckled. "They couldn't even handle him as a baby. I need someone to handle a man."

"I've sworn off man-handling," Meg said.

"Well, you know, that's good," Hades purred. "Because that's what got you into this jam in the first place, right? You sold your soul to me to save your boyfriend's life. And how did the creep thank you? By running off with some bimbo!"

Meg flushed with a mixture of pain and embarrassment as she remembered that betrayal. "Look," she said with a shrug. "I've learned my lesson, okay?"

"Which is exactly why I got a feeling you're gonna leap at my new offer," Hades replied smoothly. "You bring me the key to bringing down Wonder Boy, and I'll give you the thing that you most cherish."

Meg couldn't help it. She listened with interest.

"Your freedom."

Hope and despair warred within Meg's heart.

CHAPTER XI

"You should have been there!" Hercules told his father.

It was nighttime at the Temple of Zeus. Hercules and Pegasus were acting out his exploits for the statue of Zeus, which had once again come to life.

"I mangled the Minotaur," Hercules went on. "I grappled with the Gorgon. Just like Phil told me. I analyzed the situation, controlled my strength, and *kicked*!"

To demonstrate, he playfully kicked Pegasus into the fountain.

Hercules took a bow. "The crowd went wild."

Zeus chuckled proudly. "Ha! You're doing great, Son. You're making your old man proud."

Hercules stopped playing and stared up at his father. His eyes shone with hope. "I'm glad to hear you say that, Father. I've been waiting for this day a long time."

"Hmmm?" Zeus's brow wrinkled. "What day is that, my son?"

"The day I rejoin the gods."

Zeus sighed, and a cold wind swept through the temple. There were no special shortcuts, even for the son of Zeus.

"You've done wonderfully," Zeus told him. He cleared his throat, and gentle thunder rumbled across the sky. "But you're just not there yet. You haven't proved yourself a *true* hero."

Hercules was stunned. "But, Father!" he exclaimed. "I've beaten every single monster I've come up against! I'm the most famous person in all of Greece! Why, I'm an action figure!"

"My boy," Zeus said gently, but firmly, "I'm afraid being *famous* isn't the same as being a *true hero.*"

"What more can I do?" Hercules asked.

Zeus shook his head. "It's something you have to discover for yourself."

"But how can I?" Hercules grumbled.

"Look inside your heart...."

"Father, wait!" Hercules cried.

In a flash of lightning, Zeus's face turned to stone. He was a statue once more.

Hercules glanced around helplessly; then, frustrated, he dropped to his knees before the great statue of Zeus.

The stone temple shook as he pounded his fist on the floor.

The next day a double-decker horse-drawn cart drove past the city of Thebes's richest mansion. A sign on the cart read HERCULES LAND TOURS. A tour guide spoke into a megaphone. "And on your left is Hercules' villa...."

A few of the girls jumped off the cart and tried to climb over the walls to get inside and see their favorite star.

"Our next stop," the tour guide called out, "is the Pecs and

Flex Gift Shop where you can pick up the great hero's thirty-minute workout scroll *Buns of Bronze*."

Inside the great mansion, Hercules was posing in a lion skin for a new vase painting. He stood with his right arm holding his sword in the air, his left hand holding his shield.

But he was edgy. He found it hard to stand still.

Phil didn't seem to notice as he reminded his star hero of the day's schedule of appointments. "At one, you got a meeting with King Augeus. He's got a problem with his stables."

"Phil . . ." Hercules began.

"I told you, *don't move!*" the painter complained.

"And then at two you've got a luncheon with the DGR," Phil went on. "The Daughters of the Greek Revolution . . ."

Just then a salesman entered with a briefcase full of scrolls.

"What's your angle, Isosceles?" Phil asked.

"I represent the Artesian Water Corporation. We have a new product, and we want your boy to endorse it. Get this! Bottled water! What do you think?"

Phil frowned. "What are you? An idiot? Who's gonna buy bottled water?" Shaking his head, he went back to his list. "All right, Hercules, back to business. At three you have—"

"Phil?" Hercules interrupted. "What's the point?" He dropped his shield and sword and slumped down on a pedestal.

The painter threw up his hands. "*Aiee!* That's it!" He packed up his paints and stormed out.

Phil sighed and walked over to Hercules. "What do you

mean, 'what's the point?' You want to go to Olympus, don't you?"

"Yeah," Hercules mumbled, "but *this* stuff doesn't seem to be getting me anywhere!"

"You can't give up now!" Phil exclaimed. "I'm counting on you!"

Hercules just shook his head. "I gave it everything I had."

Phil put his arm around Hercules' broad shoulders. "Listen, kid. I've seen 'em all. And I'm telling you, this is the honest-to-Zeus truth. You've got something I've never seen before."

"Really?" Hercules asked hopefully.

Phil nodded. "I can feel it right down in these stubby bowlegs of mine. There's nothing you can't do!"

Hercules smiled a little. Maybe Phil was right. . . .

Suddenly the door burst open. A mob of teenage girls ran in.

"It's him!" one girl shouted. "Oh, I'm going to faint!"

Hercules backed away nervously as the girls surrounded him.

"I touched his elbow!" a girl shrieked.

"I got his sweatband!" another girl cried.

As the girls began to fight over the souvenir, Hercules dropped to the floor and tried to crawl away.

"Okay," Phil whispered. "Emergency Escape Plan Beta." He hurried to the door and blasted out a note on his panpipe.

The girls whirled around. When they looked back, Hercules was gone.

"There he goes," Phil cried. "On the veranda!"

In a mad rush, the girls stampeded outside, carrying Phil with them. When the door closed, one girl remained.

Meg.

She spotted Hercules' feet beneath the hem of the drapes. "Let's see," she said with a grin. "What could be behind curtain number one?" She yanked on the cord, and the drapes swished open, revealing one sheepish-looking hero.

But when he saw who had discovered him, he smiled in delight. "Meg!"

"It's all right," she assured him. "They're gone."

"Gee, it's great to see you," Hercules said. "I missed you."

"So this is what heroes do on their days off?" Meg joked.

Hercules sadly shook his head. "I'm no hero."

"Sure you are," Meg insisted. "I've seen all your vases. Everybody in Greece thinks you're the greatest thing since they put the pocket in pita."

"I know, it's crazy," Hercules said with a sigh. "You know, I can't go anywhere without being mobbed."

"You sound like you could use a break," Meg said. "Think your nanny goat would go berserk if you played hooky this afternoon?"

"Oh, gee, I don't know," Hercules answered. "Phil's got the rest of the day pretty much booked."

Meg grabbed him playfully by the tunic. "Phil, schmil! Just follow me …"

CHAPTER XII

"What a day!" Hercules said with a sigh that night as he stood in a garden with Meg. "First that restaurant by the bay. Then that Greek play..."

Two birds flew across the sky and landed in the bushes.

Meg winced as she saw the birds morph into Pain and Panic.

"Stop fooling around," Pain whispered.

"Yeah, get the goods, sister," Panic hissed.

Meg glanced at Hercules. He hadn't noticed they had company.

"I didn't know playing hooky could be so much fun," he said. He smiled down into her eyes. "Thanks, Meg."

Meg gulped. The guilt hit her in the stomach like a boxer's punch, but she worked hard to ignore it. She had a job to do, and feelings only got in the way. "Oh, don't thank me just yet."

She and Hercules sat down on the edge of the fountain. "Wonder Boy, you are perfect," Meg cooed.

Hercules blushed to the roots of his hair. "Thanks." He crossed to the fountain and skipped a stone across the waters. Stars twinkled in the water.

Hercules stared off into the distance as a shooting star arced across the night sky.

"You know, when I was a kid," Hercules said, "I would have given anything to be *exactly* like everybody else."

Meg laughed. "You mean petty and dishonest?"

"Everybody's not like that," Hercules said softly. "*You're* not like that."

Meg blushed. "How do you know what I'm like?"

Hercules gazed into her eyes. "All I know is that you're the most amazing person I've ever met."

"I bet you say that to all the girls," Meg joked.

"Those girls at the villa?" Hercules shrugged. "They don't even know me. It's funny, all my life I felt like a freak, an outsider. And now sometimes I feel like I'm just a different *kind* of freak. Sometimes I feel like I'm more alone than ever."

"Sometimes it's better to be alone," Meg said quietly. "Then nobody can hurt you."

"Meg," Hercules said, "I would never ever hurt you."

Meg couldn't meet his eyes. "And I don't want to hurt you. So let's both do ourselves a favor and stop this before we—"

Suddenly a blinding light shot down from the sky.

"All right! Break it up!" Phil shouted in his megaphone as he came barreling out of the sky on Pegasus. "I've been looking all over for you!"

"Calm down, Mutton Man," Meg said. "It was all my fault."

"You're already on my list, sister!" Phil snapped as he and Pegasus landed. "And as for you," he said to Hercules, "you're going to the stadium for the workout of your life!"

"Okay, okay." Hercules turned to Meg with a smile.

"I'm sorry—" she began.

Zeus and Hera proudly display their pride and joy—bouncing Baby Hercules.

Hades didn't come empty-handed to visit Baby Hercules, but he may leave without a finger!

The three Fates tell Hades that Zeus can be toppled, but they also warn: should Hercules fight, Hades will fail.

Overly eager to impress his trainer, Hercules pulls his bowstring back a little too enthusiastically. . . .

And before he knows it, Phil hits the bullseye.

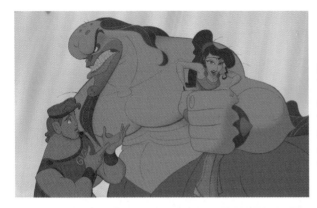

On the road to Thebes, Hercules spots Meg, his first damsel in distress, in the clutches of a wicked Centaur.

Hercules bravely attacks the mighty Centaur and frees Meg.

"So, did they give you a name to go with all those rippling pectorals?" Meg asks her rescuer.

Responding to cries of two boys who lie trapped in a cave in a rocky canyon, Hercules prepares to take action.

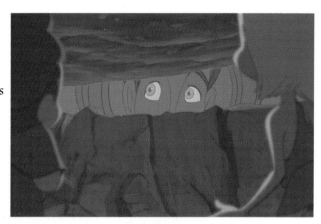

With a grunt, Hercules lifts the boulder and frees the boys—not knowing they are Pain and Panic in disguise.

Hades is proud of his helpers' stunning performance as he munches on his favorite snack—a big bowlful of juicy worms.

The Hydra is the first of many monsters that Hades sends to destroy Hercules.

Basking in the adulation Hercules receives from the villagers for saving their town, Pegasus chauffers the hero around Thebes.

"Aren't they dashing?" a mischievous Pain asks Hades, glancing down at his Herc-Air sandals.

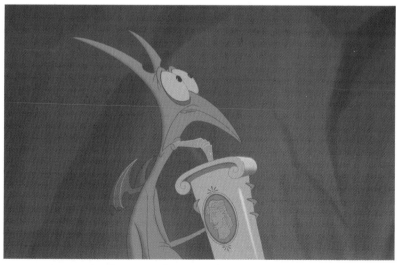

A not-so-bright Panic inflames Hades' temper by drinking nectar from his new Hercules Sports Cup.

Hercules succeeds in vanquishing the Erymanthean boar—no problem.

From a zero to a hero, Hercules proudly makes his mark among the other celebrities at the Amphitheater. But fame does not a hero make.

Meg is Hades' newest victim, but if Hercules will give up his strength, Meg will go free.

Interrupting Hercules, Hades makes him an offer he can't possibly refuse.

Shaking on the offer, a smiling Hades zaps the strength out of Hercules who is then pinned to the ground by a barbell.

In love with Herc, Meg sacrifices herself in order to keep him from harm. It is then that Hercules realizes that "a true hero isn't measured by the size of his strength, but by the strength of his heart."

"He'll get over it," Hercules assured her. "I'll see you tomorrow." He pulled down a tree branch and picked a flower. Then he gave it to Meg, along with a quick kiss on the cheek.

With a lopsided grin, he leaped onto Pegasus, and they soared off into the dark night sky.

But his mind was not on his driving. Phil climbed onto his shoulder. "Whoa! Watch it! Keep your goo-goo eyes on the—"

Thwack! A low branch knocked Phil off the horse. Hercules was so lovesick, he didn't notice and flew on without him.

Whump! Phil landed in a thorny briar patch. "That's it! We're talking curfew and a fine!" Then he passed out.

Alone in the garden, Meg sat at the edge of the fountain admiring the flower. Her heart was running like a stallion.

Suddenly fire reflected in the fountain. Meg glanced up.

Perched atop the fountain, Hades grinned at her. "What's the buzz, Meg? What's the weak link in Wonder Boy's chain?"

No way I'm going to help this guy bring Hercules down, Meg thought. "Get yourself another girl," she snapped. "I'm through."

Hades' flaming hair crackled as his face darkened in fury. "You mind running that by me again? I must have a chunk of brimstone stuck in my ear or something."

"Then read my lips—forget it." She turned to walk away.

But Hades blocked her escape. "Meg, my sweet, aren't we forgetting one teensy but ever-so-crucial little tiny detail?" And then he exploded into a wall of fire. *"I own you!"*

The noise and light woke Phil. He sat up in the bushes,

grumbling, with a big lump on his head right between his horns. But then he heard voices. Angry voices! Phil listened.

"You work for *me*!" Hades was shouting. "If I say 'sing,' you say 'name that tune!'"

Phil peered through the bushes. He couldn't believe it! There was Meg—with Hades, Pain, and Panic!

"If I say I want Wonder Boy's head on a platter, you say—"

"Medium or well-done?" Meg repeated reluctantly.

Phil smacked his fist in his hand. "I knew that dame was trouble! This is going to break the kid's heart." He raced off to tell Hercules, and so he didn't hear the rest of their conversation.

Hades put his hand to his ear. "Hear that sound? That's the sound of your *freedom* … fluttering out the window *forever*."

"I don't care!" Meg cried. "I won't help you hurt him! Besides, you can't beat him. He has no weaknesses. He's going to—"

Meg stopped in mid sentence.

Hades's smile chilled her to the bone. "I think he *does* have a weakness—*Meg*. I truly think he does." Hades snatched the flower from Meg's hand.

Instantly the blossom withered and died.

CHAPTER XIII

Oomph! Hercules landed in the sand at Olympic Stadium. Instantly he knew he had broken his previous record for the long jump. *All right!* His day with Meg had energized him. He felt like a new man.

Just then Phil entered the stadium. He looked troubled.

"Hey, Phil," Hercules called, "what happened to you?"

Phil sighed. "Kid, we gotta talk."

But Hercules didn't seem to hear. "I can't stop thinking about Meg! Isn't she the most amazing girl you ever met?"

"Oh, yeah," Phil said sarcastically. He stared up at Hercules hanging from the parallel bars. "Kid, I'm trying to talk to you! Will you come down here and listen?"

"Aw, how can I come down there when I'm feeling so up!" Hercules flipped from the bars and disappeared into the clouds.

As Pegasus watched, he was startled by a sharp whistle. At the stadium entrance a *girl* winged horse winked at him.

Pegasus chased her out of the stadium and followed her to an old barn. As soon as he went inside, the door slammed shut.

Pegasus stared in shock as the other horse split in half.

"Gotcha!" The front end of the horse turned into Panic, the

rear end into Pain.

Uh-oh . . . Pegasus thought as the two demons grabbed him.

Back at the stadium Phil was having a hard time telling Hercules what he'd overheard between Meg and Hades.

"If it wasn't for you," Hercules said, "I would have never met her. I owe you big time, little guy." He began sparring playfully with his friend.

"Will you knock it off?" Phil complained. "Listen, she's—"

"A dream come true?" Herc asked, dancing around. "More beautiful than Aphrodite? The most wonderful—"

Phil couldn't take it anymore. *"She's a fraud!"* he yelled.

Hercules stumbled backwards as if he'd been punched.

"She's been playing you for a sap," Phil added.

"Come on, Phil, stop kidding around. I *love* her!"

Nose-to-nose now, Phil yelled back, "She *don't* love you! She's nothing but a a two-timing, no-good, lying—"

"Shut up!" Hercules roared. He gave Phil a poke. *Pow!* The force sent Phil flying into a pile of gym equipment.

"Okay, that's it! You won't face the truth? Fine." Phil untangled himself and stormed out of the stadium.

"Phil, wait!" Hercules cried. "Where are you going?"

Phil turned long enough to shout, "I'm going home!"

"Fine! *Go!* I don't need you!" Hercules answered.

"I thought you were going to be the all-time champ," Phil muttered sadly as he left. "Not the all-time *chump.*"

"What got his goat?" a strange voice asked.

Hercules glanced up. A man with flaming hair perched atop the goalpost. Smiling, he did a perfect back flip off the bar. "Name is Hades. Lord of the Dead. Hi. How you doing?"

"Not now, okay?" Hercules started to leave.

But Hades swooped down to block his move. "Hey, I'm a fast talker. See, I've got this major deal in the works. And Herc—may I call you Herc?—you keep getting in my way."

Hercules shoved him aside. "You've got the wrong guy."

"Just hear me out, okay? I would be *eternally* grateful if you'd just take a day off from all this hero business. Monsters, natural disasters ... *Pffft!* They can wait a day, okay?"

"You're out of your mind!" Hercules strode off across the field.

"Not so fast," Hades called out to him. "Because, you see, I do have a little leverage you might want to know about."

He snapped his fingers.

Hercules turned around and gasped.

Meg appeared—bound in smoky chains.

"Let her go!" Hercules cried. Horrified, he lunged for her. But his hands grasped thin air. Meg had disappeared.

There she was—behind him! He grabbed again—

And she disappeared once more.

Angry, Hercules lunged at Hades, but he passed right through him—as if the mad god were a ghost.

Frantic now, Hercules shouted, "Let her go!"

Hades smiled and rubbed his fingers together in delight. "Okay, so here's the trade-off. You give up your strength for, say, the *next* twenty-four hours. And Meg here is free as a bird and safe from harm. We dance, we schmooze, we carry on, we go home happy. What do you say?"

Hercules stared Hades straight in the eye. "People are going to get hurt, aren't they?"

"Nah. . . ." Hades shook his head, then shrugged. "Well, it's a possibility. It happens. It's war. What can I tell you?" He floated closer to Hercules, his eyes dancing with fire. "But what do you owe these people, huh? Isn't Meg—little smooshy face—more important to you than they are?" With a wave of his fiery fingers, he tightened Meg's chains. She groaned in pain.

"Stop it!" Hercules cried. He stared at the god's face and knew he meant business. "You've got to swear she'll be safe."

Hades nodded. "Fine. Meg is safe—otherwise, you get your strength right back." He extended his hand. "We're done. What do you say we shake on it?"

Hercules stared at Hades' fingertips, trying to decide.

"I really don't have time to bat this around," Hades snapped. "I'm kind of on a schedule here. I've got plans for August, okay? I need an answer now." When Hercules still hesitated, he added, "Going once, going twice—"

"All right!" Reluctantly he reached for Hades' hand.

"Yes!" Hades shouted. "We're there. Bam!"

The moment their hands touched, the color began to drain from Hercules' body. He felt weak. He staggered.

"You may feel just a bit queasy," Hades noted. "It's kind of natural. Maybe you should *sit down*!" Hades tossed him a barbell.

Hercules tried to catch it, but—*Crunch*! It pinned him to the ground. He'd never felt so weak in his entire life.

"Now you know how it feels to be just like everybody else," Hades sneered.

As the sun peeked over the horizon, a chariot drawn by a large griffin thundered into Olympic Stadium, with Pain and Panic at the reins. Hades started to climb aboard, then turned back to Hercules. "One more thing. Oh, you'll love this."

He snapped his fingers, and Meg's chains disappeared.

"Meg, babe, a deal's a deal. You're off the hook. And by the way, Herc, is she not one fabulous little actress?"

"Stop it," Meg demanded.

Hercules looked confused. "What do you mean?"

Hades put his arm around Meg and grinned. "I mean, your little chicky here was working for me all the time!"

"You're—you're lying!" Hercules gasped.

Hades snickered. With a dramatic flourish he pointed to Pain and Panic. Instantly they transformed into the two little boys.

"Help!" Pain said, repeating his lines.

"Jeepers, mister, you're really strong!" Panic repeated.

The demons snorted with laughter.

Hades smiled at Meg. "Couldn't have done it without you, babe."

"No!" Meg protested. "It's not *like* that! I didn't mean—" But Hercules' look of betrayal stopped her excuses cold. Instead, she simply whispered, "I'm so sorry."

Hercules was crushed.

Pain and Panic dumped Hercu-lade over his head. "Our hero's a zero! Our hero's a zero!" they chanted gleefully.

Hades climbed into his chariot. "Hey, Jerk-ules. The next time somebody calls you a dope and a freak—believe them!"

CHAPTER XIV

High above Earth, the planets began an ancient dance the Fates had foretold eighteen years ago. The day had arrived. The planets moved into perfect alignment.

Shadows from the eclipse parted the ocean, uncovering a deep dark pit. The prison of the Titans had been revealed.

Hades smiled and drove his chariot to the sea. "Brothers! Titans! Look at you in your squalid prison. Who put you there?"

"Zeus!" they cried.

"If I let you out, what will you do?"

"Destroy him!" the Titans roared.

"Good answer!" Hades used his hand to vanquish the lightning bolts Zeus had used to cage the Titans.

The Titans marched from their prison. "Ug! Destroy Zeus—"

Hades shook his head at his witless army. "Uh, guys . . . Olympus would be *that* way."

Grunting, the Titans turned and marched off in the opposite direction. "Ug! Zeus! Destroy him!"

But Hades stopped an ugly Titan named the Cyclops, who had only one eye. "Hold it, Bright Eye. I have a special job for you."

* * *

Hermes was sleeping late, dreaming on a cloud, when something shook him awake. He glanced over the edge and gasped.

The Titans were climbing Mount Olympus!

Quickly Hermes flew on winged feet straight into the throne room to report the news to Zeus.

"Sound the alarm!" Zeus ordered Hermes.

"Gone, babe," Hermes said as he dashed out of the palace. Hovering above the city, he blew his trumpet loud and clear.

The gods grabbed their weapons, tossed on their armor, and jumped into their chariots. The Titans had to be stopped!

The city of Thebes was in flames. Its people screamed as the roar of the Cyclops struck fear in their hearts.

"I told you the end was coming," said the man who had predicted the end was near. "But *noooo*, you wouldn't listen."

"What should we do?" a thin woman cried.

"Where's Hercules?" a fat woman wailed.

Inside the stadium Hercules heard their cries for help. He heard the Cyclops scream his name. Hercules started outside.

"What are you doing?" Meg exclaimed. "Without your strength, you'll be killed!"

Hercules turned and stared sadly into her eyes. "There are worse things." Bravely he strode out to face the Cyclops.

"Look!" cried a man in the crowd. "It's Hercules!"

"Thank the gods," the fat woman exclaimed. "We're saved!"

Meg watched in horror as the Cyclops easily knocked the weakened Hercules to the ground. Then she heard a strange sound coming from the barn. She unbarred the door and hurried inside. Pegasus was tied up in ropes. He snorted when he saw Meg.

"Stop twitching!" she scolded as she struggled to untie him. "Listen, Hercules is in trouble. We've got to find Phil. He's the only one who can talk some sense into him!"

As soon as Pegasus was free, he knelt for Meg to climb on.

Meg gulped. She hated flying! But Hercules' life depended on her. Reluctantly she mounted the winged horse.

Pegasus took off like a rocket.

"Aaaaaaahhhh!" Meg shrieked as they soared across the sky.

Soon they found Phil at the dock, about to sail for home.

"Phil!" Meg shouted. "Hercules needs your help!"

"What does he need me for," Phil said, "when he's got friends like you?"

"He won't listen to me," Meg said.

"Good," Phil snapped. "He's finally learned something!"

Meg was ashamed, but she pressed on. "I know what I did was wrong, but this isn't about me. It's about him."

"Hey, shorty," the boat captain called out to Phil. "Make up your mind. We ain't got all day."

Phil put one hoof into the boat, determined to go.

Meg stopped him. "Hercules gave us something we both lost—hope! Now he's lost his hope! You're the only one who can give it back to him! If you don't help him now, Phil, he'll die!"

71

Nearly all the gods on Mount Olympus had been captured. The Titans stormed into the throne room.

The Lava Titan belched—and thick red gooey lava swirled around Zeus, covering him to his waist.

The Ice Titan blew—and the hot lava cooled into cement.

Zeus was trapped! He struggled as the freezing lava rose up around him, then stopped when he saw another uninvited guest.

Hades, Lord of the Dead, god of the Underworld, rode his chariot into the throne room.

"Flea!" The Cyclops sneered at his puny opponent and punched him one more time, sending him flying into a pillar. The pillar crashed around him. He was surrounded by rubble.

"Hercules!"

Hercules shook his head. He thought he'd just heard Phil call his name. But Phil must be long gone by now.

"Hercules!"

Hercules peered up. It wasn't his imagination. Phil and Meg flew in on Pegasus. As soon as the winged horse landed, Phil hopped off and ran to Hercules' side.

"Come on, kid," Phil coached him. "Fight back! You can take this bum. This guy's a pushover! Look at him!"

Hercules shook his head. "You were right all along, Phil." He glanced at Meg. "Dreams are for rookies."

"No, kid," Phil said, shaking his shoulders. "Giving up is for rookies! I came back because I'm not quittin' on you. I'm willin' to go the distance. How about you?"

Before Hercules could answer, the Cyclops grabbed him again. With a grunt, he lifted the faded hero.

Giving up—that would be the easiest thing to do, Hercules thought. Just let this one-eyed monster do me in.

But Phil's words rang in his heart: "Giving up is for rookies." . . . "Fight back!". . . . "I'm willing to go the distance. How about you?"

Hercules grabbed a burning stick of wood. With determination, he jammed the fiery stick toward the monster's eye.

The Cyclops dropped Hercules, who fell to the ground and then rolled to the side. Spying a rope, he quickly wrapped it around the moaning monster's ankles.

"I kill you!" the Cyclops roared, groping blindly. But as he tried to walk forward, his bound ankles made him trip. The Cyclops plunged off a nearby cliff.

Hercules fell to his knees and peered down. The giant lay still at the bottom of the sea.

But when the Cyclops fell, he'd bumped into a huge column.

"Hercules!" Meg screamed. "Look out!" The column was falling toward Hercules—it was going to crush him to death!

With no thought for herself, Meg ran and shoved Hercules out of harm's way. He was safe!

But the column fell on Meg.

CHAPTER XV

"Meg!" Hercules cried. *"Noooooo!"*

Hercules rushed to her side and desperately fought to lift the heavy stone column off Meg's still body. It wouldn't budge. I won't give up, he thought. I won't quit until Meg is saved.

With a roar, Hercules lifted again, straining for that last ounce of strength that might go the distance, that might make the difference. And as sweat poured down his face and arms, something strange began to happen to him.

A light surrounded him, soft at first, then glowing brighter and brighter.

Suddenly Hercules felt strength pour into his muscles. And then he lifted the heavy stone column into the air.

Lying on the ground, the pain nearly unbearable, Meg smiled. "Hades' deal is broken. He promised I wouldn't get hurt."

Hercules tossed the pillar aside and rushed to cradle Meg in his arms. "Why did you do this? You didn't have to …"

Meg grinned. "People do crazy things when they're in love."

"Oh, Meg, " Hercules stuttered. "I—I—I—"

"Are you always this articulate?" she joked. Then she touched his cheek. "You haven't got much time. You can still stop Hades."

"I'll watch over her, kid," Phil said gently.

Reluctantly Hercules laid Meg in Phil's arms. "You're going to be all right," he told her. "I promise."

With one last look at his beloved Meg, Hercules leaped on Pegasus and streaked off into the heavens.

The captured gods of Mount Olympus moaned as Pain and Panic led them away in chains.

Inside the throne room, Zeus was up to his neck in lava. "I swear to you, Hades, when I get out of here—"

"I'm giving orders now, Bolt Boy!" Hades barked. He leaned back as his cloud formed into a reclining chair. "And I think I'm gonna like it here." He reached for a drink and took a sip.

"Don't get too comfortable, Hades!" a voice rang out.

Hades sputtered and spun around. It couldn't be! *Hercules!*

Hercules and Pegasus swooped among the gods, smashing their chains and setting them free. With a defiant yell, the gods took up their weapons against the Titans.

Hades couldn't believe it. "Get 'em!" he ordered the Titans.

The Lava Titan spewed a stream of lava at Hercules. The Ice Titan blasted him with shards of ice. Hercules dodged both.

Then Hercules ran to his father. With his bare hands, he ripped the lava prison apart.

Zeus elbowed his son. "Now watch your old man work." With practiced aim, he hurled fresh thunderbolts at the Titans.

The giants were stupid. But not that stupid. They turned and fled. Hercules and Pegasus flew after them.

Up in the heavens, the clock kept ticking. And now the planets moved out of alignment. The sun came out, casting brilliant rainbows across the sky.

Hades gasped in horror.

Hercules grabbed the Wind Titan and whirled him around like a lasso, vacuuming up the rest of the Titans. Then he hurled them out into space. No way would they ever bother his father or anyone else again.

"Thanks a ton, Wonder Boy!" Hades was running away in his chariot. "But at least I got one swell consolation prize," he sneered. "A friend of yours who's *dying* to see me...."

For a moment, Hercules frowned. What did *that* mean?

And then it hit him.

"Meg!!!"

CHAPTER XVI

The Three Fates gathered, their common eye seeing all.

Meg's life dangled by a thread.

Atropos slowly raised her scissors and—

Swish!—cut Meg's Thread of Life.

In the city of Thebes, a tear ran down Phil's cheek as he felt Meg's hand go limp.

Hercules raced down through the clouds at dizzying speed. As soon as Pegasus's hooves hit the ground, Herc leaped off and ran to Meg's side.

He froze when he saw her lifeless form lying in Phil's arms.

Phil looked up and sadly shook his head.

"Meg! No!" Hercules cried.

No! It couldn't be! It was all a big mistake!

Gently Hercules picked her up. Her head lolled backward, and her body sagged in his arms.

With tears in his eyes, he lowered his head and kissed her one last time.

Phil laid a gentle hand on Hercules' shoulder. "I'm sorry, kid. But there's some things you just can't change."

Suddenly Hercules' sad, tear-stained face turned hard

and icy cold. "Yes, I can."

He rose and strode to Pegasus.

Down in the Underworld, blasts of fire burst out of the skull's eye sockets.

Pain and Panic scurried around the room.

"We were so close. So close!" Hades ranted. "We trip at the finish line. Why? Because our little Nut-Meg has to go all noble on us...."

Suddenly a huge rumble shook the walls and floor.

Boom!

The gates of Hades' throne room burst open.

Hercules rode in on Cerberus, Hades' gigantic three-headed watchdog. "Where's Meg?" he demanded.

"Wonder Boy, you are too much!" Hades replied. "Ya know, nobody's ever visited me here by *choice*."

"Let her go!"

"Get a grip," Hades said. "Come here, let me show you around." To Pain and Panic, he added, "Guys, get the pooch outta here before he ruins the furniture."

Nervously they approached the huge dog.

Then Hades smiled at Hercules and led him toward a giant stone doorway.

The door opened, and Hercules gasped. Inside swirled an endless vortex of moaning spirits—the river of death—heading toward a giant skull-like opening in the distance.

Meg's soul floated along with them.

Hades pretended to be surprised. "Well, well. It's a small

Underworld after all, huh?"

"Meg!" Hercules cried. Without thinking he reached into the swirling mass.

Then jerked back in horror.

His strong muscular hand had aged fifty years!

"No, no, no," Hades scolded as if he were talking to a baby. "Mustn't touch. You see, Meg's running with a new crowd these days. And not a very lively one at that."

Hercules thought quickly. "You like making deals."

Hades shrugged.

"Take me in Meg's place."

Hades' eyes lit up. "Hmm ... the son of my most hated rival trapped forever in the river of death?"

"Going once ..." Hercules began.

"Hmm," Hades wondered, "is there a downside to this?"

"Going twice—"

"Okay, okay!" Hades exclaimed. "You get her out—she goes, you stay."

Without another thought Hercules dived into the swirling vortex of souls.

Hades was shocked and pleased. "You know what skipped my mind?" he added, though Hercules could no longer hear him. "You'll be dead before you can get her out. Is that a problem?" He chuckled darkly. "It's not a problem for me!"

As Hades watched in delight, Hercules began to age.

The Fates lifted Hercules' Thread of Life ...

Hercules spotted Meg, and even as he aged, he hurried to catch up with her.

The Fates lifted the scissors up to the Thread…

Close to death now, Hercules was almost a skeleton. He reached out with his bony hand and grabbed Meg.

Swish! The Fates snapped the scissors.

CHAPTER XVII

"What's the matter with these scissors?" Lachesis complained.

"The thread won't cut!" Atropos griped.

Hercules' skeletonlike hands and arms held Meg close. But suddenly his arms began to feel stronger. The wrinkles faded away. His whole body grew younger and stronger.

A godlike glow encircled him, as it had when he was a child.

Looking through the doorway, Hades gasped. "This is not possible!" he shrieked. "You can't be alive! You'd have to be—"

"A god?" Pain and Panic shrieked at the same time.

Hercules smiled and carried Meg out of the vortex.

But Hades blocked his path. "Hercules! Stop! You can't do this to me!"

In response, Hercules backhanded Hades across the face with his left fist.

"Okay, ha, okay, well, I deserved that." Hades rubbed the side of his face. "But, Herc, can we talk? God to god? Come over here. Your dad—he's a fun guy, right? He can take a joke. I bet if you put in a good word … he'd …"

Hercules stared at Hades with ice-cold eyes.

Realizing the danger of his situation, Hades trembled and

fell to his knees. "I'm begging you—on my knees. Your dad, Zeus, like maybe he'll blow this one off?"

Hercules did not respond.

In one final, desperate measure to save himself, Hades placed his hands on Meg's lifeless form and began to plead furiously with her spirit. "Meg! Meg, talk to him," Hades begged, teetering nervously on the edge of the River of Death.

Hercules scowled at Hades' futile attempt. Fueled by his love for Meg, Hercules lunged toward Hades, knocking him into the dreaded River of Death with a powerful blow.

"Noooooo!" Hades wailed like a demonic baby. Slinking further into the swirling mass of spirits, Hades snarled, "Get your slimy souls off me!"

But the unrelenting spirits clutched at Hades, dragging him down further into their midst. Pain and Panic watched nervously from above the River of Death, relieved to have escaped punishment this time.

The Three Fates shrugged. "Who knew?"

Back in Thebes, Phil and Pegasus watched in amazement as Hercules carried Meg's spirit back to her lifeless body.

Seconds later Meg's eyes fluttered open. She smiled.

Phil cheered!

Pegasus gave her a big horsey lick!

Hercules pulled her to her feet and soundly kissed her.

And then lightning bolts struck the ground around them. A fluffy white cloud formed beneath their feet and slowly lifted them into the air.

Phil jumped on Pegasus and followed them into the sky.

The cloud carried Hercules and Meg all the way to Mount Olympus. It stopped at a long stairway that led to the entrance to Olympus. A row of cherubs raised their trumpets and announced Hercules' return.

Meg watched as Hercules climbed the stairs. The gods gave him a standing ovation and tossed flower petals in his path.

At last he stood before his parents, Zeus and Hera.

"Hercules," his mother said, "we're so proud of you."

Zeus slapped him on the back. "Fine work, my boy. You've done it. You're a true hero!"

"You risked everything to rescue this young woman," his mother added.

Zeus nodded. "A true hero isn't measured by the size of his strength, but by the strength of his heart."

Hercules beamed.

"Now, at last, my son," Zeus added, "you can come home."

Hercules gazed in awe as the gates of Olympus opened for him.

"Congratulations, Wonder Boy," Meg whispered to herself. "You'll make one heck of a god."

Hercules took one step forward, then gazed back at Meg. He saw her eyes brimming with tears, and his smile faded.

A jumble of feelings warred within his heart.

Finally he raised his eyes to Zeus once more. "Father," he said, his voice sure and strong. "This is the moment I've always dreamed of. But a life without Meg—even an immortal life—would be empty."

He took her hand, and Meg smiled through her tears.

"I wish to stay on Earth with her," Hercules announced. "I finally know where I belong."

Zeus was moved. He glanced at his wife, and she nodded her understanding.

His parents smiled through their tears.

They loved him enough to let him go.

Hercules embraced Meg, and all the gods cheered.

Then, together, Hercules, Meg, and Phil climbed aboard Pegasus and flew toward Earth. Toward home.

Soon they soared over the cheering crowds in Thebes. Hercules grinned and waved when he saw his adoptive parents, Alcmene and Amphitryon, cheering with the crowd.

Meg glanced up into the sky. The first stars of evening twinkled to life.

But the night sky seemed to sparkle differently tonight. She'd never seen that constellation before. Could it be new? Why, it looked like ...

Meg gasped in delight.

It looked like the portrait of a hero.

Hercules—up in lights!

"Hey!" shouted a man in the crowd as he, too, peered at the heavens. "That's Phil's boy!"

Meg nudged Hercules and pointed toward the stars.

When he saw his portrait, he grinned. What a wonderful gift. "Thanks, Dad!"

Now the stories of Hercules would always be remembered, as long as there were stars in the sky.